I Am enough

A JOURNAL

This journal is given to:

____

from

____________________.

I want you to know that:

____

____

____

____

www.ingramcontent.com/pod-product-compliance
Lightning Source LLC
Chambersburg PA
CBHW071202300726
48975CB00004B/1255